SPEED RACERS

RACING SOAP BOX DERBY STOCK CARS

John A. Torres

Enslow Publishing
101 W. 23rd Street
Suite 240
New York, NY 10011
USA
enslow.com

Published in 2018 by Enslow Publishing, LLC.
101 W. 23rd Street, Suite 240, New York, NY 10011

Copyright © 2018 by Enslow Publishing, LLC.

All rights reserved.

No part of this book may be reproduced by any means without the written permission of the publisher.

Library of Congress Cataloging-in-Publication Data

Names: Torres, John Albert, author.
Title: Racing soap box derby stock cars / John A. Torres.
Description: New York : Enslow Publishing, 2018. | Series: Speed Racers | Includes webography. | Includes bibliographical references and index.
Identifiers: LCCN 2017021473| ISBN 9780766092709 (library bound) | ISBN 9780766094208 (paperback) | ISBN 9780766094215 (6 pack)
Subjects: LCSH: Soap box derbies—Juvenile literature.
Classification: LCC GV1029.7 .T67 2018 | DDC 796.6—dc23
LC record available at https://lccn.loc.gov/2017021473

Printed in the United States of America

To Our Readers: We have done our best to make sure all websites in this book were active and appropriate when we went to press. However, the author and the publisher have no control over and assume no liability for the material available on those websites or on any websites they may link to. Any comments or suggestions can be sent by email to customerservice@enslow.com.

Photo Credits: Cover, p. 1 Brian McEntire/Shutterstock.com; pp. 4, 5, 7, 16, 26, 30, 31, 33, 35, 37, 38 Melanie Stetson Freeman/The Christian Science Monitor/Getty Images; pp. 9, 17, 20, 40 © AP Images; pp. 11, 12 Bettmann/Getty Images; pp. 14, 18 Duane Prokop/Stringer/Getty Images; p. 24 Kevin Dodge/Corbis/Getty Images; pp. 23, 28 Joe Raedle/Getty Images.

Contents

A New World Record

1

Sheri Lazowski knew it used to be a sport dominated by boys. Maybe she thought of that occasionally while getting ready for the big race. Maybe she thought about how much she had helped change all that by herself. But she certainly was not thinking of it when she climbed into her bullet-shaped soap box derby car. Her championship title and a world record were on the line.

This 2012 photograph from Derby Downs shows just how close soap box derby races can be. It looks like a dead heat!

Race Day

Having graduated to the Ultimate Speed Division, the fifteen-year-old girl squeezed into the very tight driver's compartment. It was unlike any other. She would not be sitting up with a steering wheel in her hands like in other cars and in other races that came before. No, for this race and for this car she would be lying flat on her back. Her head would point toward the rear of her car. She put on special goggles that have small mirrors, which somehow allow her to see the road. This way she would be able to steer. She looked very much like the luge racers do during the Winter Olympics and other winter sports competitions.

Not that the brown-haired girl was planning to do much steering anyway. This division and these cars would go nearly three times as fast as the normal soap box derby car, and the track was a fairly straight run. Steering too much would definitely slow her down. She explained her simple strategy to a newspaper reporter covering the race.

"Just go down straight," she smiled. "Go as straight as you can."

It was 2011, and Lazowski had been racing for only three years. But she had shocked the racing world by establishing a world record and winning the division only one year earlier. It had taken her a while to get used to these faster, sleeker cars, but going fast was how she was most comfortable.

Lazowski was the defending champion and was the one to beat. Everyone knew it and would be coming for her and racing with everything they had. After all, this was a sport where the winners and losers are separated only by hundredths of seconds. Everything had to be just right in order to get the fastest time. Even a breeze at the wrong time could affect a racer's final posted speed.

The track conditions that gorgeous sunny day were ideal. By the time many of the second heat races were run, there was already a new world record established. Lazowski's record was broken and her dream of defending her championship seemed in doubt. There was no way she would be able to break another world record, right?

With three cars racing at the same time during each heat, Kayla Albertoni was in first place. She owned the world record by making it down the 301-meter-long (0.2-mile-long) track in only 26.765 seconds. Amazingly, though, Albertoni did not hold the record for very long. It was just going to be one of those days. In the third heat, Jim Overmyer set a new record. He finished the course in 26.632 seconds, a mark he would beat during his next heat when his car crossed the finish line at 26.613 seconds.

Next it was Sheri Lazowski's turn. The pressure was mounting on the young teenager. Would she succumb to it, or would she rise above and

Racers get ready atop the hill and starting point for the All-American Soap Box Derby competition. More than four hundred racers from around the world race in this event.

make history? She pressed her body down in her slender car that looked more like a missile than a racing car. The car, like all the others, was placed on a small ramp at the top of the track. When the signal sounded, she took off. The aerodynamic design and the new tires helped the car glide effortlessly down the track. It seemed to get faster with each passing second.

The Race Is On

It was evident from the start that Lazowski might be doing something very special. The car whizzed by, causing everything to be merely passing blurs. But for Sheri, the race almost seemed to be happening in

Soap Box Derby Divisions

Sheri Lazowski was the soap box derby world record holder and champion in the Ultimate Speed Division. But there are other divisions and other types of cars that fall under the category of soap box derby racing.

There are three racing divisions. The Stock Division is for beginners. It is meant for children—boys and girls—between the ages of seven and thirteen to race simple cars built from sanctioned and approved kits.

The next division is the Super Stock Car Division for boys and girls ages ten through seventeen. The kits for the cars are a little more intricate and advanced.

The final division is known as the Masters Division, and it's for boys and girls ages ten through twenty who have a lot of experience racing. The creativity and design styles vary wildly in this division as racers are encouraged to come up with their own designs.

slow motion. When she crossed the finish line, there was another new record established. She had finished the course in only 26.585 seconds! She had defended her championship and set a record at the same time. Not only that, but Sheri Lazowski had now become the first repeat winner in the competition. There was no doubt that she was at the top of her sport.

Soap Box Derby

What exactly is a soap box derby? What kinds of cars are these young people driving to championships, stardom, and world records? Well, the simple answer is that soap box derby cars are vehicles with no engines, motors, propellers, or anything else that can cause it to run. Instead, these cars run on gravity. Remember the Pinewood Derby race cars that Boy Scouts make and race every year? The concept is very similar.

Sheri Lazowski is all smiles as she poses with the trophy that is nearly as tall as she is after winning the Ultimate Speed Championship race in 2011.

These cars have to be made in a certain manner, following strict guidelines. Then they are raced on downhill racetracks and driven by young people. See? It's the gravity of running down a hill that makes the cars accelerate and reach speeds between 10 and 15 miles (16 to 24 kilometers) per hour in starter divisions and nearly 40 miles (64 km) per hour in the Ultimate Speed Divisions.

The races last only about thirty seconds each. They are held every year in officially sanctioned soap box derby race locations throughout the United States and some other countries. Then, every July, there are world championships held in Akron, Ohio, where the sport of soap box derby racing was born less than one hundred years ago. The sport allows children and teens to compete in sleek race cars that they have often helped construct. They get to feel like the race car drivers they admire so much. Thought fairly new, the popularity of soap box derby racing still elicits feelings of nostalgia while it continues to draw fans from all over the world.

2 It Starts with the Kid

We know exactly who organized the first soap box derby races and when. But, just when did the idea first take root? For many Americans, the idea of children racing in cars without engines was actually first introduced to them by the most well-known comedian of all time—Charlie Chaplin.

Chaplin, the master of silent movies, was portraying his famous and beloved character "Little Tramp" for the very first time on film. The "tramp" was a kind, caring hobo who couldn't seem to stay out of trouble. The 1914 film was titled *Kid Auto Races at Venice* and featured children racing at something called the

The All-American Soap Box Derby has been drawing crowds since the 1930s. Here, ninety thousand people watch a 1936 race.

Vanderbilt Cup. Auto racing had already become very popular, and race car drivers were idolized by many. But the thought of children racing in fast-moving cars was a new concept. The Vanderbilt Cup races featured a junior division that year but were never held again.

Summer Discovery

It wasn't until the summer of 1933 that things really started happening for the sport. In June, editors of the *Dayton Daily News* told photographer Myron Scott to go snap some photographs of children playing. He drove slowly through a little town called Oakwood where he was amazed to see a group of boys cruising down a long hill on wooden boxes attached to wheel of baby carriages. Most of the car bodies were simple orange crates and vegetable crates. The boys would use rope to help steer the vehicles on some of the more advanced models.

Scott asked the children to round up a few more friends and meet him in a few days so he could take pictures of them racing in their unique little cars. More than twelve boys showed up that day with their cars, including one that reminded Scott of a soap box. While snapping his photos, Scott came up with the name the "All-American Soap Box Derby."

Suddenly all types of ideas popped into his head. He went back to the newspaper and spoke to his editor and publisher. He thought it would be a great idea to have the newspaper sponsor a series of races for kids that summer. Then, he told them, the event could grow the following year to hold a huge event that could include boys from other cities as well. They thought it was a great idea. The race that summer was successful, but it was nothing compared to what happened the next year.

In 1934, more than three hundred boys and their handmade engineless cars showed up to race. What was even more impressive was that roughly forty thousand spectators showed up as well. The winner of the first All-American race was Robert Turner, who had traveled from Muncie, Indiana, with his family to compete. His car was made from the wood of an old saloon bar. Now Myron Scott realized the sport would really take off and become something big.

A Growing Sport

The derby became too big for the city of Dayton, whose residents did not like the disruptions caused by the tens of thousands of spectators and the noise and commotion they brought. But that's when the Chevrolet Car Company, owned by General Motors, agreed to become the sponsor of the annual race.

Winning derby cars are often a big attraction for those curious about the sport. This is a 1933 soap box car raced by Bob Garvett.

Myron Scott's Other Claim to Fame

The *Dayton Daily News* photographer, considered to be the father of soap box derby racing, is actually also very famous for something else he did. It was 1952, and Scott was working for Chevrolet. Executives and marketing people were having a tough time naming their new European-styled, extremely fast sports car. They wanted it to start with the letter C and not be an animal. Names like Champion and Celestial were considered and rejected. That night, Scott found the name Corvette in his dictionary. It referred to a small, fast type of warship. The rest is history. The man who founded the soap box derby also named the Corvette!

General Motors moved the event to nearby Akron, in part because the city was home to several large tire companies and there were also a lot of good long hilly roads that could be used for racing. But the event continued growing, and soon Akron's leaders and newspapers began lobbying for the creation of a permanent home and state-of-the-art racetrack for the event. It wasn't long before the Derby Downs racetrack was built as the permanent home for the All-American Soap Box Derby in the southeast section of Akron.

An Accident and a Broadcast

Sometimes the public is fascinated by accidents and mishaps, and some people credit a 1935 accident with actually helping the sport grow. One of the racers lost control of his car, and it went flying off the track. The car slammed right into NBC radio commentator and sportscaster Graham McNamee while he was on the air. Incredibly, McNamee continued his broadcast. He even finished the event before going to the hospital, where he stayed for two weeks for his injuries and a concussion. He eventually made a full recovery.

There was something magical and innocent about the sport. People were drawn to watching young children, only boys at this time, race in their

Soap box derby racing used to be only for boys. But now girls are as involved as their counterparts. And, as you can see from this photograph, being nervous before a race affects boys and girls alike.

homemade cars. People loved to watch the races on newsreels, which were shown in movie theaters and on television. They became especially popular to watch during the tough days of World War II when American forces and their allies were at war with Nazi Germany and Imperial Japan.

The sport became an escape. Even though the annual races were stopped for the war, they picked up again in 1946 and were as popular as ever. It was if they had never stopped at all. The races have been held at Derby Downs ever since, and girls were finally admitted and allowed to race starting in 1971.

3 Champion Racers

Like every sport, soap box derby racing heroes have left their mark on the sport. But, of course, where there are heroes, there are also usually villains. Let's talk about some of the heroes first.

Hall of Famers

There is no shortage of soap box derby heroes. In fact, the All-American Soap Box Derby started a Hall of Fame in 1997 to honor the pioneers and champions of youth car racing. Naturally, the first person inducted was Myron Scott, the photographer who basically founded the sport. Inducted alongside Scott was Jim

Schlemmer. He was the sports editor of the *Akron Beacon Journal* newspaper. His words, articles, and influence were instrumental in helping secure a permanent place—Derby Downs—for the annual championship races.

Interestingly enough, another name among the first-year Hall of Fame inductees is one that most adults would recognize: Jimmy Stewart. That's right! Academy Award-winning actor and world-famous movie star Jimmy Stewart was one of the early supporters of soap box

The grandstand sign at the FirstEnergy All-American Soap Box Derby at Derby Downs Racetrack announces where the action is. Thousands of people make the trip every year to watch the races.

derby racing. The actor, who died in 1997, was best known for his movies *It's a Wonderful Life*, *Mr. Smith Goes to Washington*, and *The Philadelphia Story.*

In 1947, Stewart actually canceled the weekend performances of a Broadway show he was starring in. He reimbursed all tickets holders with his own money, simply because he wanted to attend the event. One year when Stewart was unable to attend, he convinced fellow Hollywood movie star and future president of the United States Ronald Reagan to take his place.

It's the kind of sport or activity that really hooks you once you get involved. Just ask Hall of Fame member Jack Morran. As a little boy in 1940 and 1941, Morran competed in the Akron local soap box derby. After World War II ended and racing resumed, he was too old to keep competing. So, he began volunteering in 1950 as a local track worker and then later as a car inspector. Morran eventually became the derby program's chief inspector in the mid-1970s. He is also one of the people responsible for helping to develop the program's original kit car division.

Celebrity Sightings

During its heyday, celebrities flocked to the annual All-American Soap box Derby. While movie star Jimmy Stewart may have been the first big name to support the activity, he certainly was not the only celebrity to take part.

Baseball Hall of Fame pitcher Dizzy Dean and the entire St. Louis Cardinals baseball team showed up one year to watch. Other athletes to attend included National Football League quarterbacks Otto Graham and Joe Namath, boxing champion Jack Dempsey, and National Basketball Association star Cazzie Russell. NASCAR racing legend Dale Earnhardt also attended the event.

Some of the famous actors to attend include John Travolta and Art Carney, among many other celebrities.

Jimmy Stewart loved watching the races so much that he attended the annual event six times between 1947 and 1957. In fact, one year he even interrupted his honeymoon to attend the event with his new bride, Gloria.

Today's Heroes

Some of the modern-day heroes of the sport include people like Jerry Pearson. The father of future champion racers and world-record holders raced in Kokomo, Indiana, from 1969 to 1973. Once his daughters became old enough to race, he became involved in the sport again, by designing and building cars for his girls.

In 2004, Pearson's daughter Hillary won first place and a scholarship using a car her father had modified for her. Because his daughter was one of the taller racers, standing at 5-foot-9-inches (175 centimeters), Pearson said he had to modify the brakes and steering contraptions to accommodate his daughter. Of course the cars are sent ahead so that inspectors can check them out and ensure that everyone has a fair chance at winning. Her winning car is now on display at the All-American Soap Box Derby Museum in Akron, Ohio.

Breaking the Racing Rules

Of course, for all those who work hard and strive to win fair and square, there will always be those who try to take shortcuts. In 1973, wealthy businessman Robert Lange wanted his nephew Jimmy Gronen to win so badly that he tinkered with his car illegally. Gronen, only fourteen years old, was winning every heat. But what tipped off race officials was that his heat times were getting slower and slower. Normally the very opposite is true.

Derby officials made Gronen change his tires after they discovered chemicals had been applied to the rubber. But that was nothing compared to what they found when they X-rayed his car. There was a large electromagnet in the nose of the car that actually helped pull the car as a type of motor. Gronen would activate the power source by leaning his helmet against a part of the car that had a steel paddle in it. The problem was that the electromagnet would lose power the more it was used. That's why Gronen's times were getting slower and slower.

Even though many people suspected him of cheating, Gronen was crowned the winner of the competition. Naturally he was disqualified after the X-ray results were in, and the second-place finisher was named the champion. Lange, who was Gronen's legal guardian, was charged with contributing to the delinquency of a minor. He paid a $2,000 fine. Unfortunately the scandal caused the sport to lose popularity in the family's hometown of Boulder, Colorado. Two years later, there were no more races there.

4 So, You Wanna Race?

Does soap box derby racing sound like it's for you? Are you ready to get involved with thousands of other young people your age? Before getting started, there are a few things to consider. How involved do you want to get? In other words, do you see yourself competing in local races and then trying to qualify for the All-American Derby during the summer? Or do you just want to see what it's like to glide down a long hill in a soap box car to experience the thrilling power of gravity in an engineless car? Whatever your level of commitment or interest, there is no denying that the first thing anyone needs to do is build a derby car.

Soap box derby racing is a great opportunity for parents to bond with and spend quality time with their children interested in racing.

Building a Derby Car

According to just about everyone who has raced, building the car is as much fun as getting to race it. First you need to determine what kind of car you'll need to build. The first kind of car to build is the soap box derby stock car. This is for the Stock Car Division for boys and girls ages seven through thirteen.

The racer in a stock car cannot weigh more than 125 pounds (57 kilograms). The reason for this is that the entire weight of the car plus the driver cannot be heavier than 200 pounds (91 kg), and the car itself weighs about 70 pounds (32 kg). Because the races rely on gravity as the cars coast down hills, the heavier a car is the faster it can go. Also, these racers should not be much taller than 5 feet, 3 inches (160 cm).

Now, of course, if racers weigh less than 200 pounds (91 kg), they are allowed to add weights to the car to get it as close to the 200-pound maximum weight as they can. Stock cars are typically red, white, or blue.

The Super Stock Car Division is for more experienced and older racers from ages nine to eighteen. These cars weigh about 73 pounds (33 kg) and cannot exceed 240 pounds (109 kg). That means the driver cannot weigh more than 150 pounds (68 kg). The car is sleeker than the stock car and is known as a lean forward design.

The third and final car design is the Masters Car used to race in the Masters Division. The Masters Division is for experienced racers between ten and twenty years old. This is the heaviest car of the three, weighing in around 88 pounds (40 kg). Racers can weigh as much as 160 pounds (72 kg). The total combined weight of car and racer cannot be heavier than 255 pounds (116 kg).

The design for this car is a bullet-shaped vehicle. The driver lies down inside of it, becoming nearly enclosed. The car should be able to accommodate racers up to six feet tall.

All soap box derby cars must be weighed with their driver before being allowed to compete.

Ultimate Speed Challenge Cars

The first year of the Ultimate Speed Challenge was 2004. This racing division, sanctioned by the All-American Soap Box Derby, is meant to excite and inspire ingenuity and different designs. It's the only division without a super-strict guide on what the cars need to look like.

Because of the open rules, over the years there have been many different and sometimes zany car designs. There are also very few limits on what types of wheels and tires can be used. Even the use of solvents that make tires bigger is allowed.

There is a rulebook and very explicit specifications on how the cars need to be built. You can choose to follow these guidelines and build your own car with your own materials, or you can purchase a car kit.

Car Kits

Each different division features a pre-fabricated car kit that takes between four to six hours to build. The only items not included in the kit are the racing wheels and any added weights you might need to make it as heavy as legally possible.

The cars are not allowed to be painted so you must use a pre-painted shell on your car.

Now, it's important to understand that for most racers—particularly the younger ones—a parent, guardian, or mentor is expected to help in constructing the soap box derby racer. But the rules specifically state that the adult should not simply build the car for the racer; he or she should help only when necessary. The idea is to let the children build as much of the cars as they can. The cars and the car kits are equipped with all the same parts and items. What makes one car different from another is the inclusion or exclusion of optional items that are clearly listed in the instructional manual as optional.

In addition to the wheels and weights, the only other items not included with the kits are the tools needed to put it all together. Here is a list of the tools needed for assembling a car: Phillips screwdriver, flathead screwdriver, set of open wrenches or socket wrenches, standard pliers, wire cutters, Allen wrench, tape measure, hammer, masking tape, electrical tape, and contact cement. Some optional tools that might prove helpful in the construction of the cars include automotive wax, soldering gun, power drill, C clamps, and Tung oil.

Don't blink or you might miss the action. These two soap box derby cars are whizzing by in a blur of speed.

The cars are made of wood with metal washers, bolts, and other metal hardware pieces. The hardware can never be covered by putty because race inspectors need to be able to see them at all times. The provided shell then fits neatly over the body.

You may be unsure about some assembly rules. Can you move the car's brake pedal to the other side? What type of contact cement and wood filler are you allowed to use? Exactly where can you place the weights? Don't worry; everything is specifically spelled out in the rule book.

So, ready to get started? Now all you need to do is find a club or a race in your area.

Rules, Races, and Clubs

5

You've built your derby car with the assistance of a parent, guardian, or mentor, and you feel comfortable trying out your vehicle on hills in the area. You feel safe and confident. Now what?

Well, you've gotten involved because ultimately you don't just want to take the car down hills by yourself. You want to see how your creation and racing skills stack up against other drivers about your age. There are many types of soap box or car box racing clubs throughout the country. Luckily, the All-American Soap Box Derby program has local races all over the country

After being weighed, soap box derby cars are lined up in a secure location ensuring that no one tinkers with them before the races.

nearly all year long—weather permitting of course. And there are lots of clubs. The All-American Soap Box Derby is the only program with the annual championship in Akron, Ohio. It has become very famous over the years.

Race Locations

One rule, however, is that racers absolutely have to race in the race city closest to where they live. Any winner of a local race—dubbed a "local champion"—is allowed to travel to Akron, Ohio, and compete in the annual All-American Soap Box Derby World Championship. There, they compete against other local champions.

There are also several clubs and race organizations around the world in countries such as Canada, the Philippines, Japan, and New Zealand. Of course, the sport of soap box racing is practiced in many other countries around the world including as far away as Australia. But the countries mentioned are officially sanctioned with the All-American Soap Box Derby program.

In all, there are more than one hundred sanctioned race locations around the world.

How to Find a Race Near You

In the age of the internet, just about anything can be found online, including where to go and race your newly built soap box derby car. But, if you are interested in competing in sanctioned races in order to go for the All-American Soap Box Derby Championship, then you'll need to find out what region you live in and find the closest club to you.

There are twelve racing regions in the United States, and they are broken down geographically. For example, the states of Mississippi, Georgia, Alabama, and Florida are all located in one region. This means that young people from these states would compete against each other in local races. Check the websites at the end of this book for this type of information.

A racer scrunches way down at the starting line as she gets ready to race.

Rally Race Program

Now, so you don't get bored racing at the same tracks within the same club and against many of the same racers, there is another awesome program offered to all the fledgling race car drivers. It is called the Rally Race Program, and it works on a point system. Rally Races are offered throughout the United States and Canada. Racers can earn points depending on where they finish in certain Rally Races. The Rally Racing season goes from Memorial Day to Memorial Day, and the drivers with the most points earn the title of Rally regional champion.

Racers are allowed to race in as many Rally Races as they want to during the course of a season. The Rally Regional Champions—the top point-getters—are then invited to race against other Rally Regional Champions at the annual All-American Soap Box Derby World Championships.

In addition to the Rally Regional Champions, any Rally racer who has accumulated 180 points or more is eligible to compete in the world championships as well. How do you accumulate 180 points without being a Rally Racer Champion? Well, point totals are earned depending on your finish in a race. For example, those who win a race earn forty points. Second-place finishers get thirty-five points and third-place finishers earn thirty points. This continues all the way down to the eight-place finisher, who gets five points.

A racer who has never finished in first place but who comes in second place for five races and in eighth place for another would have exactly 180 points.

Rules and Safety

Now, you've got your car and you've found your local race club. The next thing to do is to familiarize yourself with the rules. Every club has a copy of the rule book, or you can view it online. The nice thing about the rule book is that it starts out with and stresses throughout the importance of good sportsmanship and fair play.

Safety is the most important factor to consider when derby car racing. Two of the most important essentials are a helmet and goggles.

Many of the clubs also list the many benefits of becoming involved in soap box derby racing. These include leadership development, family engagement and enrichment, honesty, integrity, and perseverance, as well as teamwork and collaboration.

The rule book is easy to read. Take the time to learn the rules in order to avoid embarrassment or disqualification from a competition. The main rule to understand, and it is written in bold print so you cannot miss it, is that every single racer must agree to have his or her car inspected by sanctioned race officials before every race.

The other matter that is stressed is that of safety. The idea of soap box derby racing is for everyone to have fun and experience the thrill of competition. The last thing anyone wants is for someone to get hurt. For that reason, racers must all wear helmets—at every race level and age—and the helmets must all be issued by the All-American Soap Box Derby. That is also the reason why race inspectors must check everything from car weight to steering to brakes.

Of course, there are many other soap box car organizations. One, for example, is called the American Boxcar Racing International Club. Its stated goal, as is the case with many of the other clubs, is to bring families together to enjoy wholesome and fun activities and to teach young people about teamwork and sportsmanship. There are even some clubs that are geared for adults where the total weight of the car plus the driver cannot exceed 500 pounds (227 kg).

6 The Future of the Sport

So, is there a strong future for a sport or recreational activity like soap box derby racing? After all, box cars or soap box cars are a nostalgic nod to our past and even to the days of our grandparents. With so much competition in today's world for our attention, can this wholesome, outdoor activity compete against video games, computers, tablets, smartphones, and other activities that young people enjoy?

It is nearly a photo finish as the checkered flag is waved, signaling the end of this soap box derby race.

While there are some healthy indications that the sport is doing great and thriving, such as the uptick in local races throughout the year, there is also some concern that interest might be starting to wane. For example, in 2017 the All-American Soap Box Derby had to cancel the Ultimate Speed Division because of a lack of racers entered into the division. But, much like the ever-popular Pinewood Derby, it is hard to imagine the sport of soap box racing ever really going away.

The Pinewood Derby

Anyone who ever spent any time in or around the Boy Scouts of America program knows a thing or two about the annual Pinewood Derby. This activity was started by Don Murphy in 1953 and has never slowed down. It involves scouts making a small, hand-held car out of a simple uniform block of pine wood.

Cars can be any design at all, painted and decorated, but they must be a certain weight in order to race. The car races down a simple track. Most Pinewood Derby cars are not allowed to weigh more than five ounces.

The annual races are normally the highlight of most Boy Scout troops and dens, as the young people compete to come up with the most daring designs and the fastest cars.

The Tradition Lives On

In recent years, the All-American Soap Box Derby board of directors has had to make some tough decisions to save money as the nation's economy soured. That has caused some to wonder about the future of soap box derby racing. But there have been some heroes who have stepped forward, like actor Corbin Bernsen, who helped put together a film about the sport and is donating all the proceeds to try to save it. Other celebrities have also stepped forward to try to help. They promote the wholesomeness and fun of derby racing.

Mallory Bruen won the Super Stock Division of the FirstEnergy All-American Soap Box Derby in 2016. The FirstEnergy sponsorship was welcome news to everyone involved with derby racing.

But more recently, we have started to see some signs that the sport may be bouncing back. Certain companies, such as Red Bull and the FirstEnergy Corporation, have purchased sponsorships and attached their name to certain races. This has brought in much-needed revenue.

Innovations and Partnerships

There has also been talk about expanding the age range for racers who can compete as well as increasing some of the weight limitations so that some older kids might stay involved longer. Also, the organization has introduced an educational program to schools where teachers use the derby-car construction as a way to teach math, engineering, and science skills. The program began with just two cars in one Akron, Ohio, school but has since expanded to include about 250 cars in numerous schools that cover eleven states. That, according to derby officials, has helped increase the sale of derby car kits by a whopping 40 percent.

It was the partnership with the schools that also attracted the attention of professors with the University of Akron. And in 2017, the president of the university made an exciting announcement that the university's college of engineering would be partnering with the Soap Box Derby in what many believe will be a real boon to both the derby and the school.

The reason given by school officials for the partnership is to promote something called STEM, which stands for science, technology, engineering, and math. The partnership is called Zipping Towards STEM. It involves university engineering students working with eighth-grade teachers in their classrooms to help teach kids about the design process and the engineering principles involved in building the cars.

In another part of the partnership, university freshmen will build and design their own cars and compete against other engineering schools in a new event at the annual championship races. This partnership is sure to bring more exposure to the sport of soap box derby racing and likely attract more interest among casual fans and families.

The partnership is being viewed as a "win-win." While it just may save soap box derby racing by getting more kids involved, it will undoubtedly help the university as well by helping more and more children learn about the fun stuff you can do in engineering and science. After all, if you can build a car without an engine than can travel 30 miles (48 km) per hour, then you can do many more things.

"We look forward to exposing more students to our STEM-based education programs through our collaboration," said Soap Box Derby vice president Bobby Dinkins in a press release announcing the exciting partnership. "We've partnered with the College of Engineering on several projects recently and feel this is a perfect fit because so many of the kids who become involved with Soap Box Derby racing are future engineers."

A Bright Future

The future of soap box derby racing looks to be on the upswing and heading back to being on solid ground. And that can only be a good thing for families looking to spend more time together out of their homes and away from the televisions and computers that tend to dominate our time. Remember, this is an activity that was founded in good, old-fashioned, wholesome fun by a photographer whose simple task one summer afternoon was to take photographs of children having fun.

Are you ready to give it a try?

Glossary

commotion A noisy or confusing uproar.

electromagnet A piece of metal turned into a magnet by passing electricity through it.

fledgling Someone inexperienced at a new task.

integrity The quality of being good, honest, fair, and decent.

mishap An unlucky setback.

modified Changed from its original intent or design.

nostalgia A feeling of longing for or thinking of the good times in the past.

prefabricated Consisting of sections that are already put together to allow for easy assembly.

proceeds Money taken in from sales of an item.

reimbursed Paid back for money spent.

sanctioned Officially approved of.

sleeker Smoother and glossier than other items.

soldering gun A pistol-shaped electric tool that applies hot tin to form a mechanical bond between items.

STEM The term given to the all-around study of science, technology, engineering, and math.

succumb To give in and stop resisting.

Further Reading

Books

Fulton, David. *Winning Ingredients: Aerodynamics, Energy, Weight, Suspension, Alignment, Precisions, Decision, and Construction*. Amazon Publishing, 2013.

Lambert, Ron. *Racing the Wind: Spending Our Youth in Small-Town America*. Columbus, TX: Printer's Guild Publishing, 2014.

Reed, Ronald. *Derby Downs: The 1936 and 1937 All-American Soap Box Derby*. iUniverse Publishing, 2014.

Reed, Ronald. *Tallmadge Hill: The Story of the 1935 All-American Soap Box Derby*. iUniverse Publishing, 2013.

Websites

THE ALL-AMERICAN SOAP BOX DERBY

soapboxderby.org

The official home of the All-American Soap Box Derby.

HOW TO FIND A RACE IN YOUR AREA

soapboxderby.org/aasbd-race-program/local-race-program.aspx

A list of regions, clubs, and upcoming races to join.

NATIONAL DERBY ASSOCIATION

ndr.org

The official home of a national soap box derby association.